TO: McKenna

Xmas 2022

FROM: Great Auntie Karen and
Great Uncle Rich
with love ♡

For Mom and Dad, who taught me to work hard and dream big.

—EG

This book is for all children, even if have they have grown up.

—ET

Copyright © 2020 by Sourcebooks
Text by Erin Guendelsberger
Illustrations by Elizaveta Tretyakova
Endsheet texture image by design cuts
Cover and internal design © 2020 by Sourcebooks

Sourcebooks and the colophon are registered trademarks of Sourcebooks.

The full color art was created in Adobe Photoshop with a Wacom tablet.

Published by Sourcebooks Wonderland, an imprint of Sourcebooks Kids
P.O. Box 4410, Naperville, Illinois 60567–4410
(630) 961-3900
sourcebookskids.com

Library of Congress Cataloging-in-Publication Data is on file with the publisher.

Source of Production: 1010 Printing Asia Limited, Kwun Tong, Hong Kong, China
Date of Production: March 2022
Run Number: 5025819

Printed and bound in China.
OGP 10 9 8 7 6

Little Red Sleigh

words by Erin Guendelsberger

pictures by Elizaveta Tretyakova

 sourcebooks
wonderland

In a quiet corner of a cozy Christmas shop, there was a little red sleigh as bright as Christmas morning. She wasn't very big, and she wasn't very fast, and she was very young for a sleigh.

But deep inside her strong, sweet heart, Little Red had a big dream.

She longed to become Santa's big red sleigh.

Everyone in the shop told Little Red that her dream would never come true. It was impossible! She was too small, too slow, and much too young. She couldn't fly, they said, so how could she possibly be Santa's sleigh?

Little Red wondered if these things might be true... Was she too small? Too slow? Too young?

But she believed, deep in her heart, she *could* fly! Through the sky, she would soar like a bird! She could *learn* anything. She could *be* anything!

And this Christmas, she was going to prove it. She would travel to the top of the world, find Santa Claus, and show everyone what she was made of.

So, as winter fell, Little Red went north.

Her journey was very difficult. She dragged herself through mud and grime. She crossed rickety bridges and braved treacherous paths.

Soon, she started to worry she wouldn't make it to the North Pole before Christmas.

Then, she found some train tracks.

"Where are you headed?" asked a friendly train.

"The North Pole," said Little Red.

"Off to see the Big Man, huh? Well, climb aboard!" puffed Train.

Little Red hopped onto the train, and they chugged quickly down the line.

"You have so many cars!" Little Red said. "I wish I were as big and fast as you."

"I wasn't always so big or so fast," said Train. "When I started out, I had just two stock cars. I worked up and down these tracks for a long time before they gave me a third. Then I earned a fourth, a fifth, and so on."

"Oh, I can't *wait* to be as big as you," said Little Red.

Train laughed. "Be patient, little sleigh. Life builds up one car at a time."

As they steamed north, the
ground gradually changed
from softly rolling hills…

to vast, icy mountains.

After many, many miles,
Train slowed down and
stopped at a station.

"This is as far as I go," he said. "But over that ledge, you'll find Yellow Truck, who can help you go farther."

"Oh, thank you!" said Little Red.

As she slid over the hill, she saw a bright yellow truck loaded with Christmas trees.

"Hello!" said the little red sleigh. "Can you show me the way to the North Pole?"

"Happy to," Yellow Truck said. "I'm heading that way myself, to deliver these Christmas trees to the Big Man. Hop on!"

In the truck, Little Red snuggled between trees, surrounded by the sweet scent of pine. Yellow Truck drove down a narrow road—rounding curves, dodging holes, and gliding smoothly over bumps.

"Wow!" said Little Red. "I wish I could drive like you do."

"Well now," Yellow Truck said, "I wasn't always so. Used to be, no one thought I could make deliveries. Then one winter, I took a load of trees up north. It was just a few. But the next time I got more trees, then more and more. Life seems to build up one tree at a time."

That afternoon, snow began to fall. Ice covered
the roads. Yellow Truck's tires slipped and slid.
His windshield wipers ran faster and faster as the
snow fell harder and harder.

"We have to pull over," hollered Yellow Truck.
Little Red could barely hear him through the
whipping wind. She closed her eyes and held tight.
She feared that if she flew off, she would be lost.
Then she would never find the North Pole!

When they stopped, Little Red carefully opened her eyes. Snow was still swirling, but through it, she saw lights twinkling red, green, blue, and white. Was this the North Pole? Had they finally made it?

"Do you see Santa Claus?" asked Little Red. She strained her eyes but could see nothing through the blur of falling snow.

"I'm sorry," said Yellow Truck. "We didn't make it to the North Pole. We'll have to stay here until the storm lets up."

Little Red nestled deep into the bed of Christmas trees, thankful for the shelter. But as she watched the snow pile up and up, her heart felt heavy. She'd come so far, and it was nearly Christmas. How would she ever get to the North Pole now?

Little Red fell asleep sniffling and wishing for Santa.

In the morning, the sun rose high and bright. The storm was over!

"Happy Christmas Eve!" Little Red said. "Will we get moving soon to deliver the trees in time?"

"Afraid not," said Yellow Truck. "My tires are stuck tight. I can't go anywhere today. But you should take a look at the town, I'll keep an eye on you from here. You never know what you'll find when you look around someplace new."

Little Red thanked Yellow Truck and slid off the trees, out of the back, and down the street. She hadn't gone very far when a pair of mittened hands suddenly picked her up.

"Oh, wow! A sleigh!" A little girl in a purple parka hugged Little Red to her chest and held on tightly as she ran down the street and up to the top of a hill. The girl sat on Little Red, and then…

Little Red was just the right size for the little girl.

Together they flew down the hill again and again, sledding through the snow. Soon, other children joined in. Little Red played all day, helping each child soar through the air, watching their faces light up with joy.

"This is what it feels like to fly! I'm doing it!" said Little Red, her heart bursting with pride.

At suppertime, the girl in the purple parka brought Little Red back home. When Little Red closed her eyes that night, at the end of Christmas Eve, she felt like she was still flying.

The next day, on Christmas morning, Little Red woke up and sighed. She hadn't made it to the North Pole. She hadn't met Santa Claus. And now, it was too late.

Little Red was so disappointed. She started to cry…

But then, she noticed a small, red envelope tucked beside her. It was addressed to her!

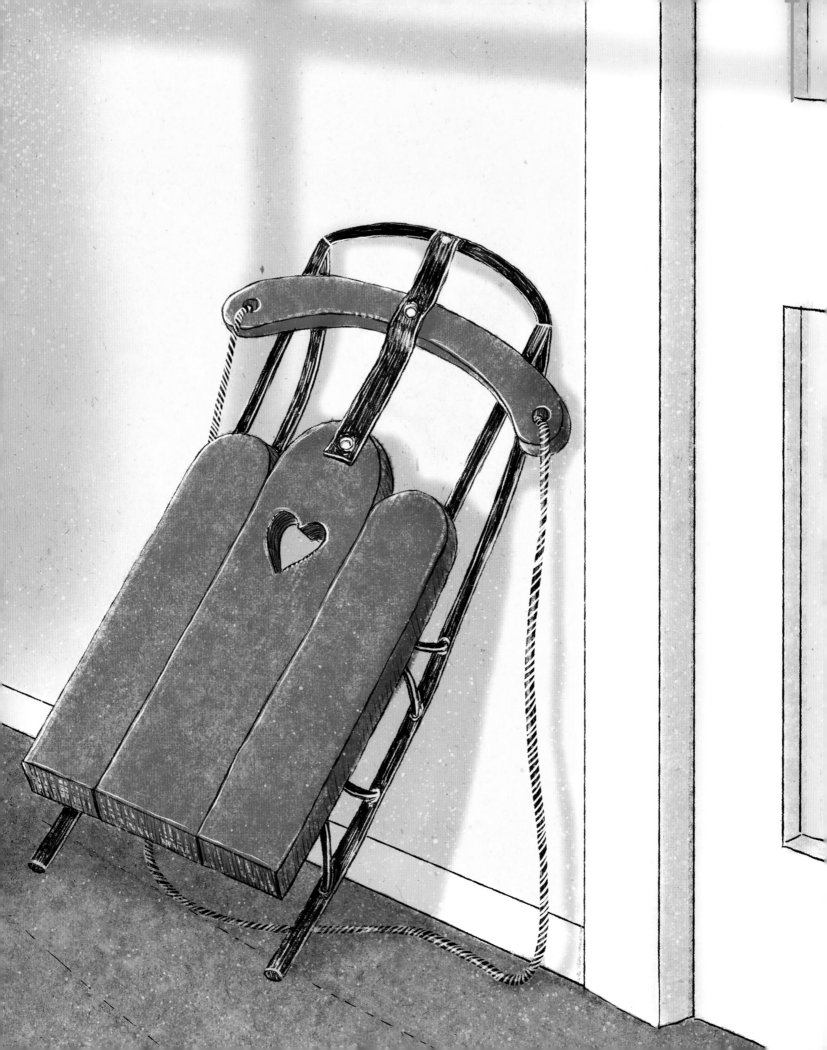

Dear Little Red,

Christmas is a time for giving. Each year, I deliver treasures to children around the world, hoping to bring them joy. But sometimes, I need a little help. Yesterday, you delivered Christmas joy to many children. Thank you so much! You made each of those children very happy, and you did it just by being yourself. You are a very special sleigh indeed.

I could really use someone like you up here in the North Pole. As a special thank-you, you are cordially invited to visit me in the North Pole next year as we prepare for the holiday.

Merry Christmas!

Love
Santa Claus

Little Red couldn't believe her eyes. The North Pole? With Santa Claus? Her dream had come true!

Just then, the little girl in the purple parka bounded down the stairs. Little Red was ready. At last she understood what she was meant to do. She would build her life up spreading joy, one child at a time.

MERRY CHRISTMAS